ALEX MORRALL

Remembering Not To Breathe

Contents

Helen & The Grandbees-READING BOOK SIGN UP

Buy Alex Morrall's Debut Novel "Helen and the Grandbees"
"Uplifting" by the UK national press,
"Breathtaking" by Awais Khan.
Read it here: mybook.to/HelenandtheGrandbees

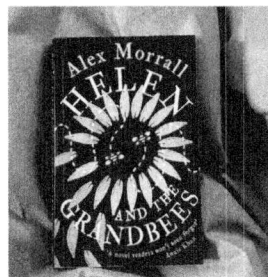

Twenty years ago, Helen is forced to give up her newborn baby, Lily. Now living alone in her small flat, there is a knock at the door and her bee, her Lily, is standing in front of her.

Reuniting means the world to them both, but Lily has questions. Lots of them. Questions that Helen is unwilling to answer. In turn, when it's clear her grandbees are in danger, tangled up in her daughter's damaging relationship, Helen must find the courage to step in, confronting the fears that haunt her the most.

Told in Helen's quirky voice *Helen and the Grandbees* addresses matters of identity, race and mental illness.

READ THE FIRST THREE CHAPTERS FOR **FREE** HERE and sign up for videos, readings and updates www.alexmorrall.com/free

Snow

by

Clare Morrall

My name is Robert Anderson and I am eighteen. I am sitting between the sky and the earth, contemplating the greatest miracle of my life. Unlike my two brothers, David and Michael, I have lived through my seventeenth year and stepped over the threshold into the unexpected beyond. I don't know what to do with this future.

We lived in a small fishing village in south Devon, and spent most of our childhood watching for smugglers, searching for secret passages from our garden to the beach. We often trailed people through the village if we thought they looked suspicious - we were interested in spies.

My father went by train to Exeter every day, where he worked as a solicitor. My mother was very keen that we should be well educated. She made us sit round the wooden table in the kitchen and recite the three times tables, the fours, the fives. When I say the tables in my mind now, I can still feel the grain of the wood under my fingertips - smoothing along the grooves in time with our chanting. I was the youngest, but I could beat the others easily. I liked numbers, their patterns, the rhythms that they set up in my head.

David, my oldest brother, wasn't interested in school or the work round the kitchen table, but he was still our leader because he had the best ideas. "Let's be pirates." "Let's make a raft and take it down to the harbour." We frequently found ourselves knee-deep in water, saluting David, the captain, while our contraption of paint tins and old planks sank slowly down into the mud below.

As we got older, David taught us everything we needed to know about girls, about which pubs you could get into if you were underage, about smoking - secretly under the railway bridge at the edge of the river. I felt sick, Michael actually vomited and David laughed.

David laughed at everything. He knew thousand of jokes: *What do you do if you see a spaceman? Park, man, park.* He told them with a seriousness that confused people at first. They would watch his face, waiting for a signal from him, not sure for a few seconds if he had finished. Then they realised how funny the joke was.

David laughed too much. He was the first to go.

On bad days, there's a hammer inside my head, tapping into me, weakening me. I huddle into my coat of ever greater weight, keep my head down and observe others from behind a thick curtain. They never approach me because I am unapproachable. I know I am unapproachable because they never come near me. It's a circle I can't break.

* * *

You read about these things in the paper. A short headline: "Teenager drowns on Devon coast." Four or five lines of explanation. I often read these little comments now, because I know that there are people behind the words, families who will never be normal again. I think of the parents when they first hear the news, see how the mother understands first, how she grabs a younger brother and holds him tight, forcing him to change the words, making him admit it is all a joke. It isn't a joke. It never is.

I imagine the father finally understanding the enormity of what the brothers are saying:

"We must ring the coastguard."

"Take us to the place where he fell in."

But the coastguard would be too late. I knew that.

We were playing on the rocks. The tide was high and banging violently into a kind of funnel between the rocks. We dared each other to go closer to the edge, along a row of rocks that we knew were there, concealed by the rushing white-churned water. David was always ahead of us, laughing at our fear.

"Go on," he shouted to Michael, who was cautious and easily frightened. "You can go further than that."

Michael tried, but he couldn't do it. He came back and clung to the edge, his dark curly hair wet and plastered to his head. I thought he might be crying, but couldn't be sure. There was so much spray from the waves, and it was hard to know if the wailing came from Michael or the gulls swooping above us.

I saw it happen. I was trying again, following David over the sea-weed covered rocks, hearing him calling me - well, only seeing it, because it was too difficult trying to separate any individual sound from the roaring, battering scream of the sea. One minute he was there, struggling to hold his balance, laughing, laughing - then he was gone.

I stood still, watching the space where he had been, thinking he was pretending, waiting to hear his voice again. A gigantic wave roared into the funnel, churned into white foam and sucked itself out again. The next wave was already building up outside, preparing to overwhelm the outgoing water. I turned to Michael, thinking David had somehow passed me and slipped back to the beach.

Michael was looking at me, his eyes wild with panic, and I knew that I had seen correctly. I ran back along the rocks, hearing David laugh somewhere in the wind. David, our captain -

Then I saw him, just for a second as one wave sucked outwards, just before the next one came crashing down. I saw his face under the water, white with staring eyes. Then he turned into the wave and a hand lifted briefly out of the water, an unintentional goodbye.

Michael and I waited there for a long time, wanting to catch sight of him again, on our hands and knees trying to reach down into the water to find him. I looked to Michael to tell me what to do. He was two years older than me and I was too frightened to make any decisions. When we realised that we couldn't reach David any more, Michael told me to run home for help.

"I'll stay here," he shouted above the wind. "Just in case."

* * *

My school sent me to a doctor after Michael died. They said I was too silent, and under-achieving. I went willingly, wanting to shed a few pounds of my guilt. The burden of my survival sat heavily on my shoulders. I didn't expect to get rid of it all, but a bit would have been nice, so that I could edge past the evergrowing obstacles in my mind.

I was sent to see a Dr Palmer. He tried to lead me down a corridor of doors, through the murmur of voices, into a place humming with deep thoughts. He was a nice man, going bald on top. When he walked, his legs seemed rubbery, bending at the knees, and he lurched from side to side like a clown. I liked him. We sat for long hours, studying each other and I couldn't speak. When people find out about my brothers, they don't know what to say, it's hard for them to take. But I realised Dr Palmer was different and needed me to tell him about them. I didn't want to disappoint him. I wanted to explain about David and Michael, about how my father disappeared as well one day, unable to cope any more. I wanted to tell him about my mother - how she fussed over me, overfed me, put me to bed if I had a cold and waited for me to sneak up on my eighteenth birthday, the cut-off point in our family, expecting an accident every minute of the day. Every time I breathed, she heard asthma. If I was late home, I would find her wandering through the village calling my name. I woke up once, in the middle of the night and found her leaning over me, listening to my breathing, checking I was still alive. Every step I took, she was behind me, watching my feet move, waiting for me to fall down an unexpected trapdoor.

Dr Palmer would have listened if I'd told him this. There were lines round his eyes from smiling - but I thought he looked tired. I was worried the story of my life might turn out to be too much for him. I didn't know how to put it into words. I thought of several openings: "My two brothers died when they were seventeen;" "My mother expects me to die at sixteen"; "I'm trapped - I can't breathe." But I couldn't say them. They got stuck before they reached my mouth, so we just sat and nearly smiled at each other. Sometimes, he would talk and I answered with a nod or shake of the head. There was too much silence in me - I couldn't reach down far enough to bring out what he wanted. Maybe I'll do it better when I'm older.

* * *

I clean telephone boxes. It's good work. They give me a car and I work through the night when the phone boxes are empty. There aren't as many now as there used to be, so I have to drive long distances to reach them. I don't often go home any more. I work till dawn, then park in a quiet layby and sleep for a few hours in the car. I carry a sleeping bag and a pillow. It's quite comfortable - the front seat folds down to make a bed.

I like the phone boxes at night. They have their own individual lights, so they look comfortable and welcoming in the dark. People leave behind amazing things - purses, umbrellas, books, credit cards, odd shoes, bottles of pills. Why do they use phone boxes? Don't they have mobiles? I have one. I can be contacted at any time of the day. "Robert? Emergency. Someone's been sick in the box at the corner of Dart Street and Darlington Crescent."

It makes me feel important. Trouble with phone boxes? Call Robert Anderson, and here I am within the hour. The Flying Phone Box Cleaner. I never need to see people. I live in my own world. Nobody comes near me. My only contact is electronic. There's nobody behind me, watching the way I walk, seeing a limp when there isn't one, predicting disaster every minute of the day. Nobody to give me Lem-Sip if I sniff, or Vitamin C because I look peaky. Now I turn round and I'm alone. I can cough if I want to and there is no spoon waiting with the Benylin.

* * *

Two years after David drowned, Michael reached seventeen. My mother had already become peculiar. She sometimes forgot that she'd fed us and two hours after supper we would be summoned for a second supply of cottage pie and apple crumble. Michael and I sulked and argued. My father sat at the table and pretended that we hadn't already eaten. He hardly never spoke.

My mother never stopped speaking. She chattered on and on without saying anything. Michael and I would kick each other under the table and out-stare each other, while she talked and interrupted herself with outbursts of hysterical giggles.

"Your father's always loved my bacon and egg pie you know – or was it the steak and kidney? There again, it could have been cheese and onion – well, it was one or the other – he still does, of course – " She was like a bird, twittering and fluttering, never still.

"Nice crumble," my father would say after our second sitting and then he would go to his study. He spent most of his time in his study now, but I don't know what he did there. The phone never rang and he never used it. His silence settled round him like a blanket of snow and we could none of us get more than three feet near him.

Michael's seventeenth birthday came and went. It was his year, the year he would make a mark on the world. We were all watching and waiting. He was the older brother now, but he didn't want to be. He wouldn't go anywhere with me. He told me to get lost. He liked to go out and come home after midnight. I think he drank. Nobody ever told him off.

* * *

Extraordinary disasters occasionally get a mention on the Ten O'Clock News, although they usually prefer to have more than one person dead. It can be your moment of glory, your only chance of fame if you can die in an unusual way. Although you're too dead to enjoy it. I know there are statistics. You are more likely to die in a road accident than to catch AIDS. More likely to die of a heart attack than to drown at sea. More likely to lose a leg than to be struck by lightning. Life is full of hidden dangers. It's a wonder that any of us survive at all. And whatever the odds, a few privileged people get struck by lightning. Someone goes out into the middle of a football pitch in an electric storm and doesn't bother to lie down. So the lightning gets him.

I was there with Michael for once. We were with a group of lads playing football, and when the storm started, we all ran for cover under a bus shelter. We laughed and roared and pretended we weren't frightened, but Michael didn't come with us. I saw him running around in the rain, shouting as if he knew what was going to happen. I like to think he was yelling, "Come and get me!" because that would mean he had a spark of defiance in his last few seconds. It is more likely that he was cursing us all, and David in particular, for the humiliation and frustration of our subdued life. There was an enormous bang, and he was thrown up into the air, then discarded like a rag doll.

People don't often get killed by lightning. Only about three a year, I think. Bad luck if it's you.

* * *

My mother got even more confused about meals. Sometimes we would have three in an evening, sometimes none. Then one day, my father disappeared. He just wasn't there any more. Nobody seemed to know anything about it, not my mother, not my neighbours, not even the police. I did go and ask them, but there wasn't much they could do, they said.

So I went home to irregular meals and my mother watching my every movement. My seventeenth birthday came and went. We held our breath, touching briefly across our separate worlds. Everywhere I went, my mother was there, watching me, counting the days. I reached my eighteenth birthday and sighed with relief. But my mother had lost count. She carried on watching and feeding me. I took the job cleaning telephone boxes, and stopped going home very often, but it didn't seem to make any difference. Now when I go and see her, she is just the same.

"Now you must make sure you have enough blankets – nothing worse than being cold at night – did I tell you about my brother? Caught a chill – you'd better have another slice of treacle tart – "

Talking to me without a breath. I suspect she remains the same at all times of the day and night, cooking and chattering, looking after her image of me without noticing that I'm not actually there at all.

I haven't been through a winter on the boxes before. I've worked out routines, patterns that I can hold in my mind and keep to, so that I always know where to sleep each night. I like my job, my car, my mobile, my silence. On the first of every month, I drive up on Dartmoor. Today is the first of February. The night is very cold, and the bleakness surrounds me, becoming part of me. I settle down on my reclining car seat and pull the sleeping bag tightly round my neck. The cold cracks the air outside, and when I look up, the stars are frozen splinters of glittering light in the black curtain of the universe. I lie awake for some time and listen to the silence. Then I sleep soundly.

When I wake up, there is something different about the world. It is softer than when I went to sleep and more gentle, somehow. I sniff, trying to work out what is different. It's not so cold. I sit up curiously, realising that it is light outside, but it's a glowing luminescent light, brighter than normal.

It has been snowing for some time, and the snow is already thick, drifting against the side of the car. I push the door open with some difficulty and step out into this amazing world. I am at one of the highest points of Dartmoor that you can reach by car. I wade knee-deep through the snow and roar with joy, picking up handfuls and throwing them upwards into the path of the falling snowflakes. My voice is the only sound in this silent storm. It is a world where no one has ever been before, a world where you can do what you want - now, without thought of before or after. I sit down to look around. The snowflakes are drifting aimlessly, kinder, smoothing the landscape into a soft, benign blanket. I can see for miles in every direction, and wherever I look there is no one. I sit and breathe deeply, feeling the enormous distance between me and everyone else. They no longer exist. I am alone in the world I can stay here forever and no one will ever watch me again.

I am happy.

Chemistry

by
Alex Morrall

From a distance, perhaps Emily and I look like best friends in this shabby coffee shop. But Emily flows through life easy, while I am like a rock that the rest of the world has to work around.

Today she has me reading *Cosmopolitan* on our trip to town. I sip a coke, and she's at a frothy coffee with an Italian name. "How do you know if you have chemistry?" the glossy pages ask me. For me, Chemistry is an A level subject, full of shaded electrons and bumpy acronyms of molecules, but it means something else in the glossy magazines. There are bright shapes all over the page, like a horoscope for the twenty-first century, turning real life into maps you can follow, where you can get the answers right or wrong.

I kind of wish I was at home on my Chemistry coursework right now.

I glance up at Emily, whose smooth hair drops in swathes about her face, whose limbs appear to be carved out of pale wood. I think about telling her that someone asked me out on Saturday, a *boy* asked me out on Saturday, an exchange of three sentences that keeps circling in my mind. But Emily hangs out with me because I agree to do stuff with her, not because I have anything to say. She is unwrapping a purchase from earlier in the morning from its sellotaped tissue paper to finger it with her French manicure: a long string of beads: dyed wood separated with black beads. "Kind of hippy-ish, hmm?" she asks.

I nod.

"Like it, though." She flings it around her neck and it looks like it was made for her. Seemingly instinctively, she knots it at her cleavage.

"Knotted, un-knotted?"

I have no idea. Emily doesn't seem to notice. She looks past me and sighs. "Can't believe this dive. I need a one-way ticket outta here. We should go together, get bar work and stuff."

I have finished my coke, but my nails dig at the glass. I don't want to get bar work and stuff. I want to get straight A's and write academic papers. I try to think how to start telling her about being asked out. "I had to go the Post Office for Mum," I start to explain to Emily this story-not-a-story. Emily knows that Mum had broken her toe trying to move the washing machine, "Can you and your sister not work out how to help me here?" Mum had shouted sharply in a language we hardly use anymore, as her toe got stuck between washing machine shuffles. But she said sorry later on, when we were stuck in A&E trying to translate the doctor's and nurse's words to her.

"Oh, yeah. Sorry about your Mum," says Emily.

I'm about to continue but then there's another distraction, a wolf-whistle. I blush right down to my toes, even though I know it's not aimed at me. The same happens at school. It's always about Emily. There's a group of men on the table near the door. There are four of them in grubby T-shirts and utility trousers. Emily doesn't blush. She lifts and arm and smiles. "Hi there."

There is a general sense of approval that she has responded so positively,

"Builders," she whispers to me. I wish she hadn't spoken to them. The question of telling her about the man who asked me out is long forgotten as I sense one of the men approach. He flicks an almost pitying glance down at me as I move my head, and then back at Emily. He isn't interested in me, in my flushed face. "So are you girls going to join us for a pint?" He has soft blond hair and browned skin and if he were modelling levis, instead of standing here opposite me, I'd think he was good-looking.

"Whereabouts?" Emily asks.

"The Crown."

"The Crown?" repeats Emily in disgust. "So close and so sophisticated."

He shifts his feet. "So are you coming or not?"

"All that way? I don't think so."

I breathe out with relief, but the men don't go away. "Look we're trying to be nice." One of his friends, a younger man, comes and stands next to him. The other two on the table, go quiet. I can't put my finger on why the coffee-singed air has turned nasty.

Emily looks unperturbed, but she says nothing.

"We're buying the drinks."

Emily shrugs.

"Don't shrug at us. I don't think that's exactly polite."

I am suddenly conscious that it would be hard for us to leave the cafe if the men wanted to stop us. But I'm not sure I why they would want to do that. I feel for the phone in my pocket, the old-fashioned type, because of Mum.

Emily stretches out an arm and looks at her watch. "Oh, I suppose we have time for a couple."

How do I tell her that I don't want to go for a drink? I do not want to get trapped in a dusty threadbare pub with these people.

Emily stands and slings the strap of her bag over her shoulder. "Come on then."

The men seem surprised, but go to pick up the tabards left scrunched up on their table. Emily turns towards me and winks cheerfully. "Are we catching the bus?" She calls to them as she holds the glass door open.

The builders are still at the table, gathering their things. "The bus?" repeats the younger one, absently as he tips back his white ceramic mug.

"Yep," she says, "That one." She points across the road, where the High Street is cluttered with bus stops. She could be pointing anywhere. She puts her head out the door as I stare out trying to work out which one she means. "Quick! We're gonna miss it." I feel her pull at my arm so viciously I cannot resist, "Come *on*," and I am dragged out the door towards the road. I glance back at the builders as the door swings back behind me. Only the young one has his head up looking at us blankly, like he hasn't worked out what's going on yet.

Emily doesn't even glance as she charges in front of the pushchair crossing the pavement in our direction. It's going slow because Mum's on the phone with a polka dot case, but she still takes it from her ear to yell at us.

I stumble after Emily down the kerb in front of another bus, its headlights, the grill tearing towards us. I can't run right with my legs bent so low beneath me and Emily's hand still tight onto the collar of my blouse. I daren't look. The bus blares its horn in terror. My own terror feels just as loud. I can hardly stand upright by the time we are on the other side of the road, heart thumping, unsure if I really have made it alive, passers-by staring at me because we stand out for running or because I got in the way of the pushchair?

Emily yanks my arm again – pulling me into the depths of *New Look*. through piles of fluorescent beachwear, to the handbags section. "Keep down," she says behind a rack of phone cases, releasing my arm to push down on my head. There is an odd tone to her voice. I glance along at her and I realise she is giggling.

After a few moments trying to catch our breath, she bobs her head up. "They're not coming." She pants some more. "What do you think?"

I think I am going to die.

"Perhaps they're not that bothered." She tuts, standing and stretching out her legs. "I thought I was worth more effort than that." She looks at me and sniggers. "Fun though, yeah?"

I try to think how to sound cool, but I see she has already been distracted, inspecting a black patent handbag.

My heart's still thumping, so maybe I can tell her my story from Saturday to calm me down. I wait for my legs to steady. They are like jelly, but I can't admit it. Emily seems to have already forgotten about the builders.

"Is it a bit weird when someone likes you and you don't like them back?" I try and I look at a different handbag, a pink one, one that's close enough to keep Emily talking.

She raises one eyebrow, and tosses her head in a 'stupid question' sort of a way. "No. It's great. You have the upper hand. Why would it be weird?"

I drop the bag and move away. It's showing that my hands are still shaking. I can't exactly explain why being asked out was weird. For starters, why would the guy who asked me out like me that way anyway? No one's ever asked me out before.

Maybe I misread the conversation. Oh no, did I give him the impression I thought he was asking me out when he wasn't really? I replay in my mind again. I had met him briefly in the Post Office and then he had come past me later on his motorbike. That's part of the weirdness. He was a full on, no longer at college, bike-riding grown up. He pulled off his helmet revealing slightly scraggy longish red hair. Clean, wisping around his ears and goatie. "Umm.. come here for a second."

I frowned, but took one step closer, still a yard from the roadside.

He winced a bit, and cleared his throat. "Do you want to come for a drink with me sometime?"

I shook my head and waited.

He looked a bit confused by this. "Why not?"

Not having a good answer, I turned back on my way, marching along the road to home, until I heard the bike rev up and circle back the way it came. "Zizzie," I called, when I got back home. "Hurry up and come and help me unpack Mum's shopping," because it made me feel better about being mean to the motorcyclist to tell my little sister off.

I haven't answered Emily quickly enough and she is striding over to a rack of sunglasses. Maybe there isn't really a story to tell. It's just that nothing like that has happened to me before. "Hey, do I look sexy secretary, or what?" Emily shouts back, a tiny pair of lenses perched on her nose.

I find out that the man in the motorcycle leathers is called Dean, because I see him again outside the cash and carry. Mum asked me to buy onions, but I didn't know they came in brown or purple, and I can't decide whether to buy two loose onions or the red net bursting with their flaking skins and blackened patches, so I stand looking at the boxes on the pavement, a bit overwhelmed, and feeling a bit like I did on work experience when the head estate agent shook his head at me, 'all complex formula and no common sense'.

Dean's half wheeled the bike into the white painted box on the pavement and taken off his helmet, before I see him. He pulls off his chunky gloves and smiles. "You again."

I turn red and nod, but I'm not scared this time. The vibe is so different from with the builders.

He turns around and puts his gloves go into the shiny container over the back wheel of the bike as if that was all he was going to say, and then he turns back. "You're not that old are you?"

I shake my head, but this time I'm ashamed because I'd been thinking of how Emily might pay more attention to me if I had an older boyfriend; about how there aren't really any nice boys in class, they are all sweaty and pushy and laugh at me for being well-behaved.

"Sorry about that," he says. For the first time, I realise that he might be embarrassed too. "So, I know I'm not supposed to ask, but how old are you? You at school?" he asks and I nod, even though I want to say that I'm in sixth form, so we can at least pretend that it's okay for him to fancy me. "I'm Dean," he says.

"Ella," I tell him. "I was picking up Mum's benefits while she's broken her foot," hoping that the explanation will take away the misunderstanding. "Still helping out," I say gesturing at the single onion in my hand.

He leans down a long arm in his biker leathers and lifts a bag of onions. "You need more than one onion, you know." His eyes wrinkle. "They go in everything."

"Oh." I look down at the onion realising how pathetic it looks.

He laughs at my astonishment. "Didn't they teach you that in Food Tech?"

I shrug again. If he means some sort of cookery class, we didn't do that. I stop for a second to wonder what it would be like to kiss Dean, imagine rubbing his hair with my hand as we kiss, like they do on TV, but I don't think we really fit. He is very tall. I'm not sure why he wanted to ask me for a drink really.

I come back home swinging the blue carrier bag of onions and a lollipop for Zizzie. The washing machine is still stuck, at a diagonal, half way out of its gap where we have to lean over it to throw things into the sink and scrub them under running water. Zizzie is sitting on her knees on the kitchen top, carving graffiti into the top of the washing machine's paint with a biro. "You been good?" Mum asks as she staggers into the kitchen with her foot in a plaster like a golf club but bigger, and clumsier. and I wonder if she means I shouldn't have spent her money on the lollipop. Or maybe I shouldn't have spoken to Dean. She's always telling me to be careful of boys, especially the nice ones. And I don't know who told her about Facebook, but she warns me off boys there too. She says she is watching me.

"Zizzie shouldn't be on the work top," I start, and we both turn to look at her, the white of the lollipop rocking in the corner of her mouth. She ignores me, and Mum says nothing.

"Don't forget, I know all your secrets," Mum says, hobbling back to the TV. She always says that. But I have none. A man on a motorbike asking me out to a drink I never went on isn't much of a secret after all.

"I want to talk to you about how we behave outside school," says the headmistress who has assembled the girls only in the school gym. It's killing Ben Adams that he's left out. "He seems to think we're all going to be given free doughnuts, or something."

"No, Ella," Emily says. "It's because he thinks that we're all going to take our blouses off and compare bras." She's probably right, and I bring my arms defensively over my chest. Did Dean look at my chest? Or was it picking up grown up money in old-fashioned hand me down clothes from Mum that made him think I was older?

The Headmistress, Mrs Thompson, has a twitch in one eye. It flickers now as she looks over us with a dramatic silence. "The Police," she starts, "That is, the Police have been in touch with me regarding a most concerning matter."

The hall makes the usual tense intake of breath at the Headmistresses opening comments. We'd thought this would be about periods or deodorant, but it sounds like we're in trouble and the whole year group is going to be detained for lunchtime.

In the corner of my eye, I see Emily stretch out her legs and yawn. I hope nobody saw her. Mrs Thompson is always picking people out for their 'attitude' and you can't prove you haven't got one of those.

"There have been reports of strange men hanging around the school."

"There's strange men everywhere," mutters a voice laden with cynical doom behind me. "All men are strange." I wince, but Mrs Thompson doesn't seem to have noticed.

"At least one individual has been seen with binoculars at the fence at the back of the school."

There is an explosion of laughter, partially the relief that we are not in fact in trouble, partly the concept that a man in binoculars would go to all that trouble to worship at the fence constraining two hundred girls.

Mrs Thompson stills her face, but for the disapproving twitch. "Girls, this is a serious matter." She waits. Even Emily has lost her cool, stifling her giggles with her knuckles against her teeth. "If you see anything suspicious, around the school or home or on social media, I want you to tell a teacher, or a parent. We have emailed your parents. And please make sure that you go home in groups, if not using the school bus."

I look at Emily. "Have you seen him?' I mouth and she nods.

I stare and wait for her to add more but she doesn't. I want to ask her if he has red hair, but Emily doesn't really do two-way conversations.

I see Dean again on my way home from school. He follows me into the library almost absent-mindedly, as if it's the most normal thing in the world, and we stand in the foyer, with him passing his biking gloves from one hand to another.

He breathes the smell of the library deeply through the nose. "Oh, I remember this place."

I look around at the dusty Victorian interior, the flapping notice boards over the old iron radiators.

"Used to come study here. Dad wanted me to get into Oxford before he… well anyway I got in, you know. Geography."

I hold my folder wrapped to my body, confused about what to say to this information. It doesn't seem to add up for someone who drifts around the streets the way Dean does. He looks down at me and his face is sad. it feels like he's a twig that shot out from the tree, joyful and alive, but that landed against a wall. It makes him look younger, like a man at university, instead of someone in his mid-twenties. I could almost go out with an undergraduate. That would be really cool. "You planning to go to do university?" he asks and I nod. He sighs. "I dunno," is all he says.

"Did you get a good grade?"

He shrugs. "Dropped out. Came home. It was hard."

"But you got the grades to get in?"

"Yeah, but I mean it was hard to work out how to fit in to a new place. Oxford's weird. Everyone's supposed to know to wear a white or black bow tie even when they're only going down the pub, you know."

I don't really know, and I probably look at him for too long trying to work it out.

"They gave me student counselling, and said that it was probably dealing with my Dad's death was what made it hard. That had been ages before, like years. But they say it's like you store it all up and it all comes out when something triggers it."

I think of my Dad who never made it to England. I don't think of him often, there's no context for him here, just a flash of kind dark eyes and a moustache, callouses on his fingers.

"Bought the bike with the inheritance. Probably shouldn't have, but you know… after Oxford, well that was all I really knew to try for, to save for." He looks at the library doors as if he can see through them to the bike. I like the bike," he adds and then looks back at me. "How come you're not in uniform, anyways? Are you in the sixth form or something?"

I nod, blushing again, as he gives a sheepish smile, like he knows it would be kind of pervy to say, "legal, then," but he's thinking it in a non-pervy way. It's like the mistake in the Post Office is some sort of bond between us.

"Who was that girl I saw you hanging out with yesterday?" he says suddenly. "The hot one?"

I feel a surge of disappointment. He means Emily. He likes her now? "I need to do my homework," I say, gesturing through to the computers through the glass windows. Dean just does his shrug thing, and comes in with me.

"Do you think he'd go out with any of us, or is he after just one girl in particular, because Gemma's desperate," Megan hisses. We are sitting at computers, building excel spreadsheets to 'plan scenarios'. I find this easy, planning scenarios that you can make up yourself. Even when I was in the Post Office before I met Dean, pretending to be grown up I was collecting as much information as possible about my new surroundings: The lady in front picking her nose; the elderly man ahead with his eyes floating around the shop as if to catch someone in conversation. I knew I mustn't catch his eye. There is so much information buzzing about in a room, that sometimes you can reach the wrong conclusions. But planning scenarios epitomises this country, safety nets and savings and Post Offices. No night-time raids that come to take away your Dad to interrogate him in the middle of the night.

"What?" asks Emily who is sitting on the other side of me.

"Binocular man. Do you think he'd date Megan?" Her eyes are all alive underneath her flicky eyeliner and shiny shadowing.

I find these conversations irritating and start logging onto my email account where I find an email from Dean. He must have written it when he followed me to the library. That will be why he asked for my email address. He has sent me some stuff, about some band he knows. I click on the link and scroll through. The band are made up of pale men with straggling hair, not like the glossy popstars the girls like here. I think it fits the sad figure of Dean who tried so hard to be something specifically for his Dad, and didn't know who to be after that.

I look at the link to the lyrics which appear in a font made to look like shaky hand-writing, so that I cannot work out the words to start with. I feel a bump and smell Gemma's hair spray again. "The Durham Monsters!" she calls the name of the band. "You listen to them? Those guys are so *dirty*." She calls out, and I slam down the web page, glimpsing as I do so, a string or words that I was trying to make out. And if there's any doubt about the uneasy feeling the words give me, Hayley's confirmed it.

"They're just too grown up for you," calls Emily, but after planting her icy stare on Hayley, she glances at me a questioning look, conspiratorial. It makes me think I enjoy having a secret, and I might not tell Emily after all.

19

So Dean is a secret? I remember Mum saying, *I know all your secrets.*

Then Emily disappears. No one notices at first until we all begin to realise that certain friends of hers are being ushered away from class, each in turn with a parent hovering at the classroom window. "It's about Emily," hisses Megan when she has slid back under her desk and waited for Mr Hughes' eyes to pass over us. "She's gone missing."

Gemma turns, her ponytail swinging. "My Mum told me about it this morning. I saw her hanging out with a guy on the High Road, waaaay older than her. It's so awful."

I look at Hayley's wide brown eyes under the asymmetric fringe of her bobbed hair. I feel irritation light up. Does she know what her words really mean? What's age got to do with it? But her words open up an uncertainty within me. Who was this grown man?

I bite my tongue put look up to see that my own Mum has stepped into the classroom and heard the whole conversation. So it's my turn to be whisked out for a little chat, then. I love my Mum, but none of the other parents came this close to class.

"Silly little girls," says Mum shaking her head as the classroom door closes behind her and we are led towards the heads' offices. "All drama. They do not know what these things mean. They should have more no respect." She always understands English when it's really inconvenient. She is angry. She can't see that I have a secret growing inside of me. But still she shoots me a look as if to say, 'those 'nice' boys I warned you about.'

Dean's outside the library when I get there, the wisps of his ginger beard getting longer, and scraggier. It's like he's waiting for me, and of course he could be - I get here at the same time every day. "Hey," he calls with a half wave in his clumsy friendly way.

I pause mid-step, remembering the lyrics in the music he sent me; that someone older might have hurt Emily; of the sweaty and pushy boys at school who grab at you. I wish that life was like a graph of chemistry from *Cosmopolitan*. Then I would know the answers, be able to see if Dean is different from all of these problems that keep raining down on me. But life's not so predictable.

"Get away from me," I scowl at him. Even now I can't bring myself to yell.

Dean looks like I have thumped him. I feel sorry, but all of the things that could be true about him make me recoil at the same time. Dean doesn't say anything as I stare waiting for a reaction. And when he doesn't say anything, I walk away, just as I walked away from him on the kerbside when we first met, but this time I think I have hurt him more because I take a little bit of his story away with me.

The Lights

by
Clare Morrall

Watching the books accumulate was like watching a flood, water with nowhere to go: blocked drains, overflowing shelves, limited floor space. The piles grew before their eyes, rising with the passing of days. Lottie and Will were building inner walls, learning to be bricklayers, calculating their ability to absorb. At first, Lottie marked their progress on the door frame, a little line and the date, but they were growing too fast, well beyond her outstretched arms.

"We can't go on like this," she said.

But Will was caught in the manic grip of ultimate organisation. He was like a beaver, his nose twitching in anticipation of higher piles, greater insulation, a dam of such immense proportions that it could halt the leakage of knowledge into fresh air and oblivion. He wanted to be ready when the rechargeable batteries for electronic readers stopped working and supplies of replacements ran out.

He was concerned with size and shape. Subject matter became irrelevant. Titles had to be visible, the right way up, but that was all. The triumph of appearance over content: *Henry the Fourth part 2; The Last Train Out of Birmingham; The Hungry Caterpillar; Love on the Mediterranean; The Da Vinci Code; Princess Crocus and the Dandelions….* Greedy for space, insatiable. Only one picture remained on the wall: a portrait of Lottie's great-grandfather and great-grandmother, painted in oils between the first two world wars. They gazed out with a calm, bright-eyed optimism which appeared ridiculous from the perspective of their descendants' brave new world.

"It'll have to go," said Will.

"Over my dead body," said Lottie, standing in front of him, hands on hips, fixing him with the best Lady Hollyhock glare she could summon.

So he left the picture in place and stacked the books round it, using an illustrated volume of *Neo-Postmodern Masterpieces* to create a shelf over the top, lining up the surrounding books carefully, making sure there was no overlap on the edges. Lottie was losing track. Once they started to trail out of the living room, setting their sights on the hall, with a clear view up the stairs and into the bedroom, she realised that Will had lost it and they were doomed.

"Do you think perhaps we might have enough now?" she asked, as he started to unload a new batch from his trailer and carry them through the front door, staggering under the weight as he tried to carry too many. As over-ambitious as ever. Lacking balance.

He stopped, blinking in the cold light of the real world, his beaverish brown eyes wide with astonishment. "How can you even ask such a thing? When the electricity fails, books will be our only access to knowledge."

"The electricity won't fail. And even if it did, we'd have far bigger things on our minds. Fridges, freezers, lights. Operating theatres, schools, train signals – "

He stared at Lottie, genuinely puzzled by her lack of vision. "Are you serious? You don't think we'll need knowledge? No one will know how things work. And once they realise that they need books, they'll come knocking on our door, offering us vast riches."

Or they'll come with guns and take them anyway. "Stop worrying," said Lottie. "The lights won't go out."

Exactly how essential were *The Hungry Caterpillar* or *How to Build a Maze in Your Garden*?

*

The responsibility of it was starting to wear Will down. When Lottie woke in the middle of the night and found him standing at the window, looking towards the east, at the emptiness beyond, she knew that he was deteriorating again. She remained still and watched him, listening to his uneven breathing, hearing his inner agitation as it disturbed the rhythms of the night. She could see through the window from where she lay, the same view that was absorbing Will's attention. The moon was coating the land with silver, a cool, benign hand that knew how to stroke and smooth without causing any damage. They'd moved to Wales for the silence, away from the pressures of the city because Will had needed space, a calm environment which allowed him to breathe. It had proved to be a wise decision, but now, after a period of blissful calm, the monster of his obsession had redefined itself, grown a second head.

Lottie climbed out of bed and went over to him. She could feel his urgency, the trembling of an engine ticking over inside him, ever ready, never switched off. "Come on Mr Beaver, back to bed," she said gently. "It can wait until tomorrow."

He sighed and rested his cheek on her head. "We're going to run out of space," he said.

"We can't store all the books in the world," she said. "We must let other people share the responsibility."

"But nobody else realises how close we are to disaster."

"I'm sure they do," she said, looking through their double-glazed window at the dark, uninhabited landscape beyond the hills, where there were no lights. "You will not be the only person to have thought about it."

"We've built our whole way of life on inventions from the past, on the discoveries of clever men who died ages ago," he said. "Knowledge is accumulative, but it's not much use to us if it's stored on dead machines and nobody can remember how it all started in the first place."

"Let's worry about it in the morning," she said. "The lights will stay on for the foreseeable future."

*

He'd started off by raiding abandoned houses, holiday homes whose owners hadn't returned. It made Lottie nervous – afraid that he would get caught. How could he be so certain that no one would come to claim their possessions. But his expeditions were becoming more frequent. He was doing three journeys a day on his bicycle now, setting off as if each time would be his last, his trailer behind him, empty and ready. He would return a couple of hours later, overloaded, bent over the handlebars, straining on the pedals, barely able to pull the weight of the books: *Treasure Island, The Importance of Being Earnest, Diary of a Journeyman, Revise A-level German, The Physics of Music....*

"Where are you getting them all from?" asked Lottie eventually, after watching this intensity for several days without let-up. It was seven o'clock at night, darkness was settling in and she wanted to close the door and make the house cosy. "They're holiday homes. Who'd want A-level German when they go on holiday? I thought the idea of a holiday was to have a holiday. Not to plough through text books."

"I've found the skips," he said. "Behind the old library, where they chucked out the books when it closed. The ones on top have been damaged by the rain, but I'm going underneath, mining for gold. Nobody cares. Can you believe it? But they'll change their tune when the electricity goes off and it's too late. We'll be the ones with the bargaining power then."

"The electricity's not going to go off," said Lottie automatically. "And if it did, how would we see to read anyway? Wales isn't exactly a land of sunshine and blue skies." Was he being entirely honest with her? "They're not contaminated, are they? You haven't been - ?"

He started blinking again, twitching his lips as if there were whiskers attached. "I may be bonkers," he said, "but I'm not mad."

Tricky one, that. Lottie usually equated bonkers with mad, and she'd associate them both with Will. "I really would prefer to keep the bathroom clear." she said. They couldn't make the stairs any narrower without blocking access, and if the piles expanded upwards by only a few centimetres, stray books would tip over the banisters. There was very little space left. "What have you brought this time?"

An enormous grin spread over his face, transforming him into the easy, happy-go-lucky man that she used to know. *"Encyclopaedia Britannica,"* he said. "Thirty-two volumes. 2010. Last edition before it went digital. Give me a hand."

Lottie sighed. "Wonderful." There didn't seem to be much point in fighting him. He was carrying four volumes at a time, so she picked up three. The books were dark blue, leather-jacketed, gold-lettered, heavy with unread knowledge. Maybe they would mark a fitting end to his project. A grand finale.

"I've hit the jackpot," he said, his voice almost cracking with excitement. "The very heart of civilization."

"I know," said Lottie. "The jewel in the crown, the jam in the centre of the doughnut - oh!"

She'd caught her foot on the stair carpet, the edge that had been sticking up since they had moved here, the annoying ripped threads that Will had been promising to repair for the last six months. She staggered and dropped her three volumes, which flew through the air, straight into Will's upturned face. His books slipped out of his grasp and he stood swaying, struggling to keep his balance. Lottie tried to remain upright, groping desperately for the banisters that were hidden behind the books, but after a couple of seconds she tipped slowly over, following the books down, colliding with Will, knocking him off his feet. They tumbled down together, arms and legs tangling, bouncing against the tightly packed volumes of stories about family life in Bangladesh, fugitives who've stumbled into government conspiracies, missing children, the American Dream. The makeshift walls of books were collapsing around them, disintegrating into sharp-cornered missiles. Knees in faces, feet in stomachs, fingers in eyes –

And then the lights went out.

Thin White Bread

by

Alex Morrall

They've chucked me out of work. No, not for good, but for now. Blue-overalled Craig and his clipboard approached. "Andy, you've been here eight months."

Not a good sign, expected to be chucked for good at this point. I pulled off my hard hat and goggles. "Yes," I croaked.

"And you haven't taken any holiday, ever."

"I'm a part-timer."

"Hmm?" Craig turned the clipboard to an angle of twenty degrees and stared at it intently. "Thirty-seven hours a week, I make it. Definitely due a hol. There's laws y'know."

Hah, laws. Yep. Been discussing a few of those lately. "Why don't you admit what this is really about?"

"I'll pencil you in for the twelfth to the nineteenth… and then… let's have a catch up when you're back." I tried to breathe normally, *quietly*, unable to put up an argument even if I could think of one. 'Catch ups' don't come after 'holidays'. 'Catch ups' don't come in this job at all. Craig held his marble effect, name-engraved fountain pen above the clipboard for a few seconds, to give room for objection. But I couldn't think of any excuse as the pen came down.

So, an enforced holiday; a whole blank week to work out whose fault it was. Because it wasn't mine.

I could have gone away. No one's come to interrogate me, parting with the words, "Don't leave town," like they do in the movies. The sharpest words I ever heard were, "There's a clear 'turn off your engine' sign right where your truck was." Most of them just avoided my eye, pretended they hadn't seen me, another hi-vis automaton in a hi-vis woodland.

But I can't seem to find the energy to find anywhere to visit and end up staying at home. Already, by Wednesday, I'm having this funny feeling that I've been living on baked beans or chips for quite a while, and really should venture out there and buy some proper food. I push back the curtains and find the square is misty with people, some faces grudgingly familiar, others not. The daytime zombies of the square, the ones with no jobs, no purposes. There's a lady with a blue carrier bag, crossing to my side of the road. I think she lives on the square, a pensioner I suppose. Her name is Mandy. There's a wool shop, with a lady who smokes outside about eight times a day, and I've heard her call over, "Hello Mandy. How are you?"

And Mandy says, "Fine, thank you."

No one says, Hello Andy. I don't expect them to. The wool shop lady turns her shoulder and examines her window display of crocheted teddy bears, whenever I walk past. I've been tempted to turn back and catch the disapproving and slightly scared look she'd be giving me. I get the scared look a lot. I'm a big guy. Working on site's physical work. Teddy bear, I'd say to acquaintances. Wouldn't hurt a fly. Not intentionally.

I wonder if she knows why she should disapprove of me.

Those blue carrier bags that Mandy carries emanate from Carl's, Harmouth Green's so-called supermarket. They are probably filled with Carl's speciality stock of dirty mutated vegetables and tinned bangers and mash. Believe me, even the tins from that place are mutated. There's no chance of a healthy diet with Carl's about. I pull on a hoodie, leaving my tabard folded in the corner, and make my way down to the café instead.

In the café, I pile up the list of egg and sausages and hash browns and mushrooms and tomatoes and fried bread to the guy on the till, before I grab my seat, and pull a straggly looking *Mirror* from the seat next to me.

I glance up briefly to clock the people around me, and see Mandy at the counter. I contemplate burying my head in the paper but my need for company gets the better of me, but it's only when she has followed the queue through, come away with a thick china cup of tea in her hands and faced the tables that she registers me leaning desperately out of my seat, fishing for any sort of chat.

She is not going to catch my eye. I remove a discarded chip wrapper from the seat beside me. Disconcertingly, she ignores this and takes the seat opposite.

"Hallooo, Mandy." Now I've got her, not too sure what I can say.

"I have ordered toast. I am waiting for toast," she tells me. The fact that she sounds like a headmistress tells me she is struggling as much for conversation as I am.

I smile.

She smiles.

Outside the window, I see the number seventy-two groan past. I should get on the bus one day, and see where it takes me. Maybe it will take me back to the building site where the accident was. Maybe there will be a self-contained glimpse of time where an outcome could be changed.

Mandy's toast arrives. I smile again. This is supposed to indicate some sort of encouragement not to mind me and to eat it.

Fortunately, she seems to have no thought of minding me. She picks up her knife and slowly butters the three slices before neatly folding triangles of toast into her mouth. When she has finished, she pushes the plate to one side and lifts the mug of tea, inhaling the steam.

I wonder if I have to say anything at all here. "Pass the salt?" I try and she obliges after a moment.

I add more salt to my chips – passes the time - I put the salt down on the peeling table with panache and look up and smile at her, only to be confronted with the same serenity. After a few moments, she smiles cautiously back. Then the shadow comes up, leans against me and whispers, *how different are you from pointless drugged up Mandy?*

Which makes me want to push her and the threat of our similarities away with a waterfall of abuse. "How was your toast?" I ask politely, to block the nastiness from bubbling out of my mouth.

"It was burnt," she says like that's my fault too, and looks at me as if waiting for an acknowledgement of my guilt and a refund on behalf of the cafe. I cannot bear it any longer. This, at least, I can fix. I look down at the paper full of chips and begin wrapping it up. "Come on. Have toast at mine. It'll be tailor-made to your requirements."

She looks confused.

"Toast at mine?"

"Oh. Okay." She looks sorrowfully at the about to be abandoned cup of tea.

"I can make tea too." Umm, when did I last wash up? The place has been tidy, but since the 'holiday', I've been having trouble with time, living in some sort of storm.

Back at my place, I light the grill after taking Mandy's coat and hanging it on the corner of the front door so that it will not quite close. I hope she doesn't notice. Well, I mean, what's the likelihood? "So are you the lightly toasted type?" I call from the blue of the gas flames.

I squint at the browning slices. I unwrap my chips, to find they have gone hard with cold. I bung a few more slices under the grill.

I go back to sit down cross-legged on the floor, as Mandy has the only seat.

Whoa, what is she doing?

She has begun unbuttoning her nylon dress from her neck. Is she making a pass at me? Has a latent senility struck Mandy with an unpleasant urge? Then I see what sits at the centre of her chest. It looks like my thumb and two fingers mangled up, and I realise what is eating her up, what is making her so frail – sapping her energy. "It's not painful Just itchy, or sore if I knock it," she says. Her tone is the cheeriest I've heard since we met.

I am lost for words. I stare, and then decide that this is impolite, and look at the floor remembering there had been no marks on Carl's and Ewan's bodies when they were hauled up from the dry well. Perfect clean and dead.

No one ever told me - I mean, I hate to sound so stupid – but no one ever told me that you could see growths like this – on the outside. I thought it just showed up on the scans and things like that. It's not that I didn't know that it's – you know – it's fatal; just that I never realised how physical it is.

"Did you, umm, well, were you a smoker?" I gag with the memory of noxious fumes and what they can do.

She nods, her eyes gripping me guiltily, like a kid being told off.

"Have you been to the hospital about this?"

She looks at me. I wait for the slow cogs to work out a reply, and when nothing comes, realise that the stupidity is all mine. "Course you have." That will be the reason these people are drugging her up, nothing to do with mental illness, nothing to do with running away from guilt.

I lean back against into the chair, my head brushing some old post on the shelving behind. I am not going to ask what the doctors and nurses have said. I don't think I can ask. I don't think I can put Mandy through the effort of reply, don't think I could listen. I wonder if the vacant drugs were always needed by Mandy, or if they were a reaction to this. I guess it's not something you ask.

Mandy's eyes move from me to the kitchenette. This is smoking, blackly, even more noxious fumes – not that there's much worse we can do to Mandy, and maybe smoke inhalation would be poetic justice for me: What comes around, goes around.

"At least the toast here is more effectively burnt than the chippie's."

Suddenly my head thumps with the realisation. I just wish she would go away now. I really do. I've had enough of the dead, Carl and Ewan's bodies whole and clean in the well where I had covered inadvertently obstructed the ventilation. I can't be dealing with the nearly dead.

Mandy looks at me with disappointment, oblivious to my anger. "No burnt toast, please. No burnt toast," and her urgency strikes me in the stomach. I realise I can't push her away too. I empty the curled charcoaled remains into the bin and pull more slices from the cellophane. There's no big solution to wiping away the past, nothing I own that can repay that loss. All I have to hand is processed white bread and a grill.

A Winter's Journey

by
Clare Morrall

Beethoven Meets Schubert

Unable to attend performance. Too ill to travel. I sign my name on the bottom of the note that I've just scrawled to Carl Czerny, my old pupil. Ludwig van Beethoven. March 20th 1827. Vienna.

Anton Schindler, the ghastly, ghostly creature who hovers round me like a bluebottle, takes away the note to have it delivered and returns with a bowl of broth. Nauseating mush! All I really want is a drink, but my doctors have forbidden it. More operations, they say, no alcohol. I'm inclined to dismiss the lot of them.

Schindler is saying something, over-articulating as usual, but I'm not prepared to waste time trying to interpret the movement of his lips today so I hold out my conversation book. He dislikes writing anything down, afraid I'll add a derogatory remark next to his entry, just to annoy him. But I've seen the gleam in his eye when each book is completed. He whisks it away, saving it for his future biography, presumably, and produces another pristine version in a matter of seconds.

"Got them all squirreled away somewhere, haven't you, Schindler?" I say to him, relishing the look of perplexity on his long gloomy face as he pretends to not understand me. I suspect he tears out the pages where I've written rude comments about him. But I don't care. Not really. When I'm gone, my music will be my legacy. That's all that matters. And Schindler wouldn't argue with that. He believes in my greatness.

He eventually takes the pen and scribbles two words in the book. 'Franz Schubert.'

"Is he here?" I ask.

He nods.

Well, well. "You'd better go and check he's still there, then," I say. "Bearing in mind he ran away last time before we actually made contact. Courage is not a quality that comes naturally to him."

I've seen some of Franz Schubert's manuscripts, read through a couple of his early symphonies and a selection of songs which Schindler brought me a few months ago. To divert me, he said. Is Schubert as gifted as some are saying? The work I have seen is promising, with an enviable grasp of melody, but I can detect my influence on his work. He's competent, like several of my former pupils, but does he have that extra spark, the rare flame of divine inspiration that can be described as genius? My friends press me to name a successor, someone I could trust to continue my journey and explore new paths, but no one moves me enough. I refuse to give my approval to a composer who is merely adequate.

And anyway, what kind of a man cannot find the courage to approach his hero, if what they tell me is true and that is what I am to him? How can we be strangers when we both live in Vienna? A few years ago, he brought a piano duet he'd dedicated to me – *Variations on a French Song* – but he left before I could set eyes on him. Am I so terrifying that he can't meet me face to face?

"Aagh!" A particularly violent pain grips my stomach and I push away the broth, spilling it on my bedcover. "Schindler!"

Here he comes, reptilian as ever, removing the bowl from my grasp, mopping up the spilt liquid. I allow him to get on with it. If I am to meet the elusive Franz Schubert, I must be dignified.

Schindler ushers in Anselm Huttenbrenner and a small, chubby man - Schubert, presumably. I'm pleased to see Anselm, a charming man of great wit, who claims to be a composer, but does not possess the true hunger of a creative mind. How can a man be expected to search his soul for greatness when he is rich and works in a government office? Schubert, unsuccessfully hiding behind Anselm, has curly hair and a tall, domed forehead. He is peering round the room through round, metal-rimmed glasses, his head slightly tilted, as if he is struggling to see. His nickname is apparently *Schwammerl* – Little Mushroom. It suits him.

"Welcome to *Altes Schwarspanierhaus*," I say. "The Old House of the Black-Robed Spaniard." The name pleases me - I would like to write an opera about the sinister Spaniard, but nobody has written a libretto and I am running out of time. "Bring them chairs," I say to Schindler.

I reach out to greet Franz and he grasps my hands firmly. My fingers, where the blood can no longer reach, are icy. His are burning. Is the last of my life ebbing away into him or is he attempting to revive me?

He's trying to speak. Someone needs to point out to him that I'm deaf.

"The conversation book," I say, waving at Schindler, who, dripping with sycophancy, hands him the book and explains the situation. Schubert nods eagerly, almost snatching the book and pen from him, and starts scribbling.

His first words are disappointing: "I was in the audience on May 7th 1824 for your Ninth symphony. It was one of the most moving experiences of my life." Everyone says this. Isn't he supposed to be original?

"Thank you," I say. I have found that this is the simplest way to acknowledge praise. People want more from me, but I never know what, so I allow them to continue with their homage until they run out of words – which I can't hear anyway.

"At the time, I felt there was nothing else for us to write."

I am familiar with that fear. "There are always new ideas," I say. "I am working on a tenth symphony - "

His eyes are shining feverishly and he nods, several times. "The world will be holding its breath."

Anselm leans forward and writes. "I have in my possession two movements of one of Franz's symphonies. I think you would find them interesting."

"Only two?"

Schubert's glasses are misting over. "I meant to finish it, but another symphony distracted me. I intend to return to it."

"Bring it," I say. "We should discuss it."

34

"I would be honoured."

Anselm writes something else. "The next one, his ninth, is magnificent."

"Has it been performed?"

Schubert blushes. "It seems that neither of us can hear our own work," he writes. "I can't afford to have it performed."

"Ha! The usual problem. The public love our music, but they're not always prepared to pay for it."

"At least they appreciate your genius."

Indignation floods through me. "I think not. My last string quartets have been described as 'indecipherable, uncorrected horrors.' The public are not ready for my music."

"They're fools," he writes. "Those quartets fill me with profound joy." A thin layer of sweat covers his face, as if he has a fever.

"Are you ill?" I ask him.

"Merely exhilarated at being in your presence," he writes.

"Schindler," I call. He comes sidling up, his face creased into an obsequious smile. I loathe the man even as I depend on him. "Some wine for my guests."

Schindler glides away. He'll remember everything about this first meeting with Schubert and put it into the biography. I know how his mind works.

I'm seized by a blast of cold, a surge of pain. "Anselm," I say. "Take Franz away and bring him back tomorrow."

Anselm rises immediately, responsive to the limits of my health. Schubert stumbles unsteadily to his feet, trying to say something, but the conversation book is in my hand, so he has no alternative but to bow deeply and follow his friend out of the room.

When Schindler returns with the wine and sees that they are leaving, he follows them back out.

"Schindler!" I yell. "Bring me that wine!"

*

Later that day, Anselm delivers some of Schubert's music - not the unfinished symphony or the ninth, but the beginning of a song cycle. *Winterreise*, A Winter's Journey, a setting of poems by Muller.

I study them cautiously, with an unwillingness to believe in him. The truth is that I approach all music written by younger composers with trepidation. Am I afraid? Unwilling to admit that I could be overtaken by a fresh new mind? The world is perpetually searching for new heroes. Does Schubert want to be anointed as my successor? Does he possess the clarity of thought, the vision, the passion, to justify a blessing?

Winterriese is astonishing.

The music is as bleak as the poems, but the authenticity of the narrator's despair avoids all sentimentality. The naivety of the words is echoed by the music, simple but clever. The piano is used in a most unusual way, almost as a second voice, slipping into unexpected keys that should be unrelated but somehow are not. Repeated chords create an atmosphere of profound sadness, notes fall like frozen tears, major keys are even more melancholy than the minor as they provide the sharp sweetness of nostalgia, while ice and snow permeate every phrase. The barren landscape pushes itself into my room, into my heart, my stomach, touches the rottenness inside me and beckons me to my own winter's journey.

Schubert must be barely thirty and yet this is the mature work of a master.

*

He returns and sits before me, waiting for a verdict. His nervousness is manifested by one foot, crossed over the other, jerking compulsively, but I see something else in him - a secret joy. He knows, I think. He knows that he has produced a masterpiece.

"My songs are dark," he writes.

"You do not have to apologise to me for darkness," I say. "My world is as dark as anything else you will find on this earth."

He is not afraid to fly too close to the sun, even if the heat of that sun cannot alter his vision.

"Schindler!" I shout.

Franz's head shoots up. Schindler appears in front of me as if he has glided in on wheels. Where was he hiding? Why did I not see him skulking in the background, listening to every word? His face is without expression as he waits for my instructions.

"I wish you to bear witness," I say.

The two of them stare at me. I am enjoying my moment of drama. "You see this young man," I say, pointing at Franz Schubert.

Schindler nods. "Bow to him," I say. "He is my true successor."

Schubert's face lights up with delight. The heat of his excitement pulsates into the room, but it cannot reach the coldness of the pain in my stomach.

I am suddenly, unutterably exhausted. I wave my hands at the two of them. "Go. Go. I'm too tired. Another time, Franz, and we'll talk more."

A blast of cold air sweeps briefly from the antechamber into my room as Schubert leaves. I shiver, my bones brittle with the ache of sickness. Looking down at the street from my window, I see a small, round figure emerge from my house and gaze up at the sky with an expression of wonder.

It starts to snow.

Shouting Billy

Alex Morrall

Benjamin Acroyd has a mind that is truly great, bigger than other people's minds, bigger than the world. He worked this out years ago whilst reading in the dull grey classrooms of his teens. Everyone else was at playtime. Benjamin's Dad had been gone for three weeks at one point, a little longer than the normal period of his disappearances and Benjamin remembered that the last thing that his Dad had said to him was. "You're a great lad, Benjamin," as he glanced at the pristine 'A' splattered school report in his hands. The gas fire was on at the time, hissing and glowing. The armchair his Dad sat on was scruffy and orange. Everything was warm. Perhaps he had ruffled Benjamin's hair at the same time, but it's possible that Benjamin had added that detail in retrospect.

Benjamin hadn't thought much about it at the time, but when he realised that some things were easier for him than for his classmates, he put two and two together. Benjamin loved the books, the numbers that made him great when his Dad wasn't around to tell him so.

Benjamin's Dad had a dog called Billy. Billy was a large shouting dog with a long wide snout, that his Dad did explain the heritage of, but Benjamin really didn't care. White with brown patches was how he thought of Billy. Billy arrived at the house when Benjamin was twelve.

"Dad, he's always shouting," Benjamin complained after Billy had settled in for a couple of weeks.

Benjamin's Dad roared with laughter, spilling the tea from the mug in his hand onto the brown carpet. "It's called 'barking', son."

Benjamin gathered his shoulders around him. He knew it was called barking, but it felt like shouting, like Mr Andrews did at school because Benjamin could not hit the ball when it flew towards him in cricket.

Benjamin would try and find as much time away from the dog as he could manage which meant staying in his room where he could close the door, while his Mum or Dad were downstairs watching the TV. For some reason the walls of his woodchip bedroom were painted pale pink. There were two pieces of untreated chipboard attached against the corner that made up a desk and he would stay there with his school books each evening after dinner. Only the maths books in their floppy red covers really interested him, not those silly stories from other people's imaginations from English. The maths books opened other worlds, leaping and bounding through concepts, but all the same still sitting two-dimensionally on a dry page of black and white digits. Real magic. Sometimes he would lean his chin on the desk and look at the paper, and think how beautiful it was. He usually got splinters in his eye for doing this. He never understood why he got splinters in his eyes and not in his chin.

Benjamin's Mum had long gone. She left when he turned sixteen. When he looked back to the last time he saw her in the kitchen, her brown hair ineffectually tied back into a pony tail, and an apron with pictures of castles hanging over her neck, but untied around her waist, she was frustrated by an over-boiling pot, the smoke alarm and the oven alarm to tell her that the shepherd's pie was ready (in fact burnt). He remembered that she made some sort of reference to him being old enough to look after himself now. That must have been what she was waiting for, his turning sixteen. She must have been planning to leave them for years and knew his Dad wouldn't be able to take charge. Maybe she'd known eighteen would have been a better age to leave him, but when sixteen came around the two years felt like they'd make more difference to her than to Benjamin.

When Benjamin's Dad went off, he would leave money for food and bills and things. He was generous really, just not very organised. Occasionally he would leave a hundred pounds and be gone for a month. Other times over a thousand and be gone for the weekend. So Benjamin hoarded the days of extra cash just in case they would be followed by weeks of nothing. And after a while he worked out how to live on it very effectively.

Benjamin didn't know which one of his parents was paying the rent. It was a council estate, surely there was rent to pay. Sometimes if he woke up in the middle of the night that would be what would terrify him, that someone was at the door of his bedroom right now, about to barge in and tell him that he couldn't stay here, to get out right away with whatever possessions he could grab as he went.

But when it was daytime, Benjamin knew this was illogical.

Illogical as it was, it was another reason to hoard the money, to find something that he could think of in the middle of the night that would make it feel okay again. He never opened a bank account because a bank would need to use his address and this would be no good if he and his dad were thrown out of the house.

So Benjamin's Mum's plan seemed not too bad, except that when she made the plan, she seemed to forget all about Billy, that any dog, let alone Billy would not able to look after himself and never would be.

In the early months after her leaving, fattening Billy grew more and more fractious and Benjamin tried to get braver to face the monster. To start with he would trowel and then scrub up Billy's mess from the blue living room carpet, wishing he was locked up in his room with his numbers. He held his nose while locking Billy in the garden so that he could concentrate on the clean-up. He would need to walk out the front door for a moment or two before he could face making himself another baked beans and toast supper.

Benjamin eventually worked out that Billy was far happier and less messy when he would take him for daily walks, something that neither of his parents had managed consistently themselves. Leading arthritic Billy wobbling along the broken pavement, allowing him to 'do his business' when no one was looking so he could avoid using the poo bags, actually made Benjamin feel more relaxed. He could take time away from the books digesting what the books actually told him, playing with the ideas in his head. In fact, he realised that without the walks he was in danger of setting like Billy, who's crooked legs had taken the shape of the grubby blue dog bed by the TV. In his own way, Benjamin realised that he too could end up with a hunch he would not be able to snap out of, the hunch of a man over a chipboard desk.

And when things felt really really dull and there was nothing else, and his eyes would not stay open over an equation, Benjamin would remind himself that he had a great mind, and lift himself and carry on churning through the maths.

The refreshing air of walking Billy helped Benjamin to think up non-mathematics ideas too, and he was making a plan to be more than he was right now.

The next time that Benjamin's Dad came home in a ruffled khaki fleece, arms full of a Chinese takeaway, boxes, and bags - far too much for the two of them – Benjamin knew he would have to explain his plan to his Dad. His Dad was always telling Benjamin to get out of the kitchen because he didn't expect his son to be his servant, but showed no interest in preparing something to eat himself, so they often ended up with takeaways.

When the coffee table was full of opening steaming tin foil boxes, Benjamin said, "Dad, I'm going to leave in a few months. You'll need to find someone to look after Billy."

"You're leaving?" There was a little bit of hurt for a second in his Dad's voice which was quickly hidden.

Benjamin realised that 'leaving' is what his Mum did.

"I'm eighteen. I want to go to university in September."

His Dad's face relaxed, although it did seem strange to Benjamin that his Dad would care where Benjamin was, when his Dad was hardly around anyway.

"Ah, of course. You're a very clever young man. I'm so proud of your school reports. You must go to university." He nodded and tucked back into the garish orange sweet and sour pork, seemingly forgetting that he needed to find a solution to Billy. Then he stopped mid-mouthful. "But the fees. How will you cover the fees?"

Benjamin did not want to explain that he had saved so much money from his Dad's contributions so far, that he could cover the fees for the first year and intended to get some sort of job for living expenses. After that year, he would work something out. Maybe he would qualify for some sort of grant.

"I will sort this out for you, Benjamin. Trust your Dad," he gave Benjamin a warm wink. "I will have this sorted by the end of the week." and although the fridge was stuffed full of peking duck pancakes, and szechaun chicken, Benjamin's Dad was not there when he got up in the morning.

His Dad was still not at home the next day, which hardly surprised Benjamin, but there was a green shoe box neatly settled next to the sink in the kitchen. Benjamin cautiously lifted a corner of the lid, not knowing what to expect – new shoes, or a hedgehog, the only things he could associate with a shoe box. The box was full of fifties, and even though he counted them, Benjamin knew how many there would be, exactly the value of a year of university fees. No note. Benjamin was still not sure what was going to happen to Billy.

Benjamin didn't know how his Dad could source money like this. It was a mystery to him where the genes for his own genius came from. Perhaps from his Mum who never had a chance to use her intelligence, so taken up with battling housework that didn't seem her strong point; or maybe from his Dad, which would how he could provide a small fortune whenever it seemed necessary. Maybe he worked for the government. They needed mathematicians there, and this would explain why Benjamin didn't really know what his Dad did for a living. But he thought that his Dad would be a bit more organised if he worked for the government, even if he wasn't exactly a spy.

That was Benjamin's best theory until he undertook a search for his personal documents, for his grownup life. The house was so sparse, there weren't many places to look. But also, there was very little in the way of documents anywhere, no betting slips, no tax returns, and Benjamin concluded that his dad must be doing something illegal, burglaries or raids, explaining his long unpredictable absences. However, a small bedside table under the stairs turned out to hold his birth certificate, which he needed for his application. He read the ornate lettering his own name, followed by the information: *Father: Unknown.*

Benjamin was flummoxed for a while and sat down in the living room, where Billy landed on his feet, occasionally panting for attention. He found that he had been sitting there for quite some while, staring at an empty television, because when he recovered himself, it was dusk and earlier, when making his discovery he'd only just had his lunch.

There really appeared to be no formula to solve this conundrum. So Benjamin settled into his notes again: Fermat's Last Theorem, missing variables, and decided by the time he switched of the light that it didn't matter. It didn't change a single thing about his Dad.

Benjamin left things very late. He left talking again to his Dad to the week he was leaving. He had already packed to go and was starting to worry about what would happen if his Dad didn't come home until after he had left. Fortunately, he was feeding Billy just as he heard the key in the door. "Hi" he said as he came through the door. They didn't always acknowledge each other, but Benjamin had to start the conversation somehow. This time his Dad was carrying a crate of oranges. Benjamin looked at the splintering crate stamped with green lettering and decided not to get distracted.

"You remembered I'm going to university at the end of the week?" He was careful not to say 'leaving' again.

"Of course," although he looked a lot like he had forgotten. "That's what the oranges are for. Students need vitamin C. All getting ill with scurvy, I was reading."

"So, you've got a plan to look after Billy?"

Both men glanced down at the dog, who's chin was resting on his paws. He looked up with that mournful look that he never lost from his puppy days, as if he knew he had been forgotten.

"Oh, Benjamin. Oh, son. I've really messed up."

Where did his Dad go that he could not take Billy?

"Listen, son. I don't suppose you could take him with you?"

43

Billy was no longer looking at the two men, but at a spot on the dusty skirting rail, with the same please-don't-forsake-me eyes.

"It's just that, with my clients…"

"Clients?" asked Benjamin quickly.

"Yes, you know. The posh lot in London, need their pet's special routines maintained when they're needing to jet off at the drop of a hat and pay silly money for it…"

Benjamin decided not to rock the boat by asking for any further information.

"I just come home, and I can't be thinking of anymore… well anymore *pet* stuff."

It's more that you don't actually come home, thought Benjamin in his head. But he supposed he did not find Billy so frightening anymore, although it would be hard work trying to be a student with a large dog. He might have to rethink his accommodation.

And he realised that would be such a small favour in return for his own non-Dad's care, that he in turn could take on someone else's burden of something loved.

Remembering Not To Breathe

by
Alex Morrall

The sparkle on the ripples winks at me. Mrs Cowell tells us all to put our faces down into the water and blow bubbles. The chuddering air silvers out of my mouth and around my cheeks. She says to pull our whole heads underwater and the weight of my hair floats in strings up to the surface as I stare into the translucent blue and the grid of tiles. I wonder why I am holding my breath, and gasp in. The water charges through my nostrils. I come up choking, sick with the clear blue water that winked at me.

I come home with the terror of breathing in water, my ankle socks twisted over still wet feet, smelling the clear clean smell of chlorine, 'breeding verrucas!" says Mum. But I still get back on the coach each Tuesday, longing for the glistening blue, the distant thuds of underwater sounds. I will swim. I will touch the bottom of the pool, I will touch the deep mystery of the pool. In my dreams I visit an empty pool, climb the steel steps to the waterless floor and walk to the deep end, sliding down the slope at the halfway mark, putting my cheek down on the tiles in the centre of the empty deep.

Mrs Cowell glares at me when she sees me again, "I think you'll find you have

45

your swimming costume on back to front," and as I slink shamefully back through the plywood changing room door with the broken lock I try to tell myself it doesn't matter because I have no curves yet, nothing to see here.

Later she takes me out of the class, the width-running children, all smaller than me, all learning so young because their parents didn't have to save the pennies. She doesn't smile. She tells me off for cruising so close to the buoyed rope, like a can hold it, like it will stop me if I fall.

As she directs me along the width, I can only keep my chin out of the water with tippy-toe and doggy paddle, and she holds me with a pole with a loop around my waist and says, 'paddle', and I paddle for my life, believing and sinking, feeling the wire touch my waist all at the same time. I touch the wall of the pool. "And again," so I paddle "and kick!" and I am out of breath and trying to pull in air, or is it water? and my arms being to tire, but I manage to reach out to the opposite water, and buoy myself up when it hits me that I did not touch the floor that the second time.

This time I go back without being told, and in the middle I fall, I fall like a pencil plunging below the surface, streams of water following me down, but I remember not to breathe in this time, and I know that this is not who I really am. I know that I made the last stretch unaided and I just have to tell myself that I can. I can swim, I believe it even while I am flailing, and slowly, stretch after stretch, I stop flailing.

Now when I dream, I dream of flying. I dream that it's so easy I never understood how everyone thought it would be so hard. You just lift your arm, 'like so,' and trust the currents to take your legs in tow so you can hover over the bed, and drag yourself through the open window.

I dream of flying. In the blue.

Extract from Helen and the Grandbees

This free extract of Alex Morrall's novel "HELEN AND THE GRANDBEES" is re-printed with permission from Legend Press.

Helen

We three sat together on the sofa for two. The sofa was made of bobbling grey and white threads. The foam stuck out through the gaps on the arm on April's side. The gas fire flickered with pale blue lines. Bill was sitting closest to the black and white TV, so that when he leaned forwards to pick up his tea, I couldn't see the picture. But back then, I just didn't mind. We were warm. We were cosy. Nothing could ever hurt us while we sat here as a three. The bad stuff was yet to come.

The bad stuff. That's why I can't bear to call Bill and April Mum and Dad anymore.

Back then, April was sad. Sometimes her eyes were red. But she said, "Isn't it nice that we three can sit here on the sofa for two?" Even though there was supposed to be another one of me, another little girl. April had told me to expect her, like a present that you have to wait for and, when you're eight, waiting takes a very long time.

But the little girl that started, she dropped out earlier than she was supposed to. After that we all knew that there would not be a baby sister for me, not ever.

Instead we agreed that if there had been four of us, we definitely wouldn't have fitted on the sofa for two. We couldn't all have sat together in the back of the taxi like we did that day, to get home from my baby sister's memorial.

I learned what people do at memorials: They go to a flat field, and put flowers next to a small stone that you are not allowed to sit on. This is why Bill said that it would be sensible for April to have a memorial. Because it would be good for her and we would get to ride in a taxi. Me for the first time.

It was windy at the memorial which made me shiver, but it made April shiver even more, as if she was so so cold, as cold as you ever could be. And when I remember that bit, I think of her as my Mum all over again.

Back in the warm, we could feel safe on the sofa for two because we all fitted. We filled in all the spaces because I was still an eight-year-old girl who had had her first ride in a taxi, who wanted to sit on the memorial stone, who honestly believed it was better that there were only three. We were close. Nothing could come between us. There was never any need for there to be anybody else.

But sometimes you can be too close. Now I have grown old, I want to shout that fact back at the memory of us. We should have left more space between us on the sofa for two. We should have let other people in.

It was wrong what happened when we were too close and I have to blank my mind to forget about it.

So when I grew out of being that little girl, when I stretched into my teenage years and the world looked so different, I left the sofa for two. And when I left I made sure that no one could find me and take me back.

1. The Happy Ending

I want to hum a tune: Beep beep bop. Do you like that tune? Beep Beep Bop...

I know. I was telling you a story. I was escaping my middle-aged body, trying to remember how it was to be a child all those years ago; or forget how it was. Well, I'm getting confused from the painkillers. I am trying to remember some of my childhood, but not all of it.

And when bad things bubble up, I check out. Beep Beep Bop.

People worry about me checking out. Some people used to worry about me, once. But checking out of reality is better, safer than the day the ambulance people found me walking in the middle of the pedestrianised street, crying. I felt shame then, a different sort of shame from all the days before.

After that day, I learned how to be free of what other people thought of me, stopped worrying when people winced at my Dudley accent. Could anything be worse than being found by the ambulance men, crying in the street? I dressed my long red hair in a green turban and I stopped trying to be thin. And I wore flip flops in the winter and not just when I took the rubbish out to the bin huts that were surrounded by the fly-tipped fridges. Sometimes when I wore flip flops in the winter I maybe did care a bit about what people thought about me. I was hoping they would see me and know that I was an independent lady and I didn't need a suit and a boardroom to prove it.

I don't do that so often now, though.

I check out. Then I check back in. This is a good way of living, a simple way, checked in or checked out.

But it's all fuzzy in my head right now and that makes it harder. Checked in is here, decades after running away from home, in St Thomas's fractures ward. I am in a bed chair surrounded by wires and tubes, power sockets, monitoring lines, tubes from the dosage machine, sending strange substances into my veins and the occasional beep that is not from the tune in my head. I had an accident, a slip up. I've been feeling dizzy and tired the last few years and then I finally slipped up. I feel like I am in some science fiction series, like Blake's 7 that Mum and Dad would watch on the sofa for two. I don't even like science fiction. Maybe I knew that one day I would be here like this, hooked up to the robots that control the dose that controls the pain.

Some of the beds next to me have people sitting next to them, with hand holding and kindness. But many do not. Many have their eyes and fingers and ears hooked up to extra machines, iPads and headphones. No one seems to think it's wrong to check out of reality so long as it's with an iPad and headphones. This sort of checking out is okay. My sort of checking out has to be hidden.

Checking out isn't working so easily for me either, because with the drugs and everything, I start remembering the past, and I don't like that very much. I don't like that at all.

I spend a lot of time at St. Thomas's, even when I haven't just had a slip up, but it's the building next door I usually visit. I'll be back there next week, waiting for the bus under the grey brick of Deptford Station and the trawl through the Old Kent Road. I will ignore the man who throws chips at the back of my chair and stare out of the window through my reflection at the old seventies offices converted to churches; Georgian houses nestling between phone shops and international supermarkets; and smashed-out discount furniture stores with chipped fascias.

And I'll reach the waiting room where I can slip in and out of my realities. I will try to fill my checking out with a daydream of the hills with the wind blowing through my long red hair, my long red hair that I cut once to make out I wasn't mad. Or maybe the memories that will come back to me uninvited will be of the days when I had felt joy. Things have happened to me that I never expected to happen to me and yes, some of them even brought me joy.

So for a moment, just that thought of the wind lifting my hair behind me.

But I am already being interrupted by the commotion at the end of the ward. Some people are leaning out in their bed chairs, awakened from the hospital-reveries, to take a look at what is going on. Now that I have been disturbed, I lean forwards too. I see a young black girl at the end of the ward, striding along the beds, a hospital trolley briefly freewheeling as she pushes past it. The girl looks as if she is trying not to run. She is followed by a nurse who is trying not to look like she is chasing after her. Both are trying to look like they are not having the conversation they are having.

It's the voice I recognise first, the voice that says, so firmly, "I have a right to be here." A voice that is both a child's, but with the self-knowing of an adult. I know that voice and it's coming straight for me.

Good grief. It's Aisha.

* * *

But Lily arrived in my life before Aisha and Lily was a really good thing. Truly, if I keep beep beep bopping like this I will forget about the part of reality that turned out to be so beautiful.

After running-away-to-London, bad things happened. I was fourteen.

It was not all bad when I ran away from Dudley to the city threaded with dirty Victorian railway bridges. There were some good things: I had a nail varnish that was such an unbelievable pink. A pink that could only have existed in the nuclear age. Oh yeah, a radioactive bubble gum pink that was pure plastic.

And some mornings I would wake up, and search out the least chipped nail and stare, and delight in that pink in the daylight. It was so elegant, so modern. Wherever I happened to have woken up, in someone else's cluttered bedsit, or in the doorway of a neglected building, and however broken and bruised I was, that pink nail varnish was something familiar, like an old bedspread, like a friend. My comfort came with me wherever I woke up.

But a lot of bad things happened too, like the day that I had stinking period pain as I sat to rest on a bench at Southwark Cathedral, like my sides were about to explode for two days, and they took me to a different hospital. They gave me a bath in hospital, and they shaved me too, you know, in private places. Then they hooked up my ankles into strange metal arms.

"Breathe like this…" said the nurse who put a syringe in my leg when I was lying down, when the pains were louder and quicker. So I breathed like that during the pains. But between the pains I stared at my pink vanished nails right until the next roaring pain would come.

The nurses looked down at me as I lay on the bed like I was a piece of dirt. And I tried to be good and I tried to be quiet through the explosions but it was impossible to be even slightly quiet.

And eventually my insides ripped out into a beautiful brown little baby, bald and covered in blood, kicking angrily at the air.

Now, I do know my birds and my bees nowadays. It's just that the birds just aren't worth the mention.

Oh, but my little baby bee. You've got to believe me: she was wrinkly and whiny, but beautiful. Beautiful feet, unbelievable toes, warm black skin. I wanted kiss every single eyelash. She was more wonderful than a hundred zillion pink nail varnishes, and with a hundred zillion different perspectives to look at her cute ears and nostrils and tear ducts and wide black eyes, and grasping fingers, and her addictive love to me.

I called her Lily.

And I could only clasp her to me all the time and feed her, and wake and feed her again. And I would get up in the middle of the night in the safe little flat they had given me, a whole train ride from London Bridge with the rotting windows and rotting curtains. I was changing her and singing to her in the flat where I could not keep the dishes clean and cook and hold her. I loved her. It circled in the air that I loved her and that I needed to look after her. Properly.

But the time was so confusing. Was it day? Was it night? The fluorescent kitchen light would hum at me, and the clock leered at me... I knew I had to wash, but wash what? The curtains? The bee? The dishes? And she would scream at me, my beautiful little bee. Screaming bee.

And they took her away from me for good after three weeks. 'They', the machine, the council, hospital, social services. The System.

When the stern man with a stethoscope called me into his office and told me that my flat was not clean and that this would hurt my bee, I listened ever so carefully. I did not want my beautiful bee to have to come into hospital again.

"We have had a conference," he continued with a tone that told me I must never question, never interrupt, "And we have concluded that your baby will be safer with good parents. I mean, older parents. We can find her parents from a similar ethnic background."

Of course, this was an impossible thing. There was no such thing as a life without my baby bee now that she had arrived, just a heavy clouded sky and a concrete London. So even though I could hear the words I did not really think that they could do this. If I was just strong enough I could make this impossible thing go away. I sat crying with my hands in the lap of my floral green skirt. I counted out tear after tear making rivers down my cheeks and tickling my chin until I realised that the System was not going to change their minds no matter how much I cried. Taking Lily away was a thing that was really happening.

"Can I say good bye to her?" I croaked through the tears, but she was already being taken away.

I was allowed to stay in the two-bedroom council flat that they had given me with the lock on the front door. So when they sent me back alone from the hospital I had somewhere to hide from those ones who flatter you, then trap you. I could bolt that front door if I ever needed to, even when the local teenagers left a burning car in the cul-de-sac outside. Once I even had to let a screaming girl into the stairwell as she begged for help from an attacker on the intercom. But I was too scared to let her though my front door.

And this meant that there were no more babies.

But I didn't know how to fill two bedrooms and a sitting room and a large kitchen diner. They just made me feel lost in so much space where there was no screaming bee. I was still a little girl. I would look out of my window onto the tiny weeded gardens of little grey houses of Deptford and see more empty space. In the first week, I pushed the settee into the kitchen diner, and made that the day room. I slept in one bedroom. I never ever opened the other doors, because there was no bee inside.

My kitchen window also overlooked a small playing area, with brightly coloured climbing frames and a roundabout. In the middle of each afternoon it would fill up with lots of little girls who weren't my bee. Sometimes I would reach out my hand to the window as if I could touch their tiny images in the glass. And I would feel the cold of the glass.

I counted each year out knowing what I was missing: a little girl growing into a toddler who tried to eat yellow Lego bricks; at primary school, bright-eyed over matching stationary sets; a taller preteen who would dance to Madonna with earmuffs and a hairbrush, and have the sparkly shy eyes who looked to Mummy when her friend's parents would try to talk to her. I even wanted her to be one of the bolshy teenagers who crammed into the shiny red buses in the middle of overcast afternoons, long long after they took her away from me.

My life was a broken-up jigsaw, no roots, no branches, no sky, no ground, no horizon but the blankness never went away. And as Deptford stone-washed its railway arches and built towering flats with intercoms and glass bricks, I thought it was the end.

Beep Beep Bop. No. It wasn't the end. Although it felt like the end at the time. My beautiful bee, she was going to come back to me. She was going to look for me. Someone who didn't want to hurt me was going to look for me.

CLICK HERE to continue reading the "Uplifting" (Daily Mail) and "Engaging" Awais Khan HELEN AND THE GRANDBEES: mybook.to/Helenandthe-Grandbees

Circuit Boards

by Alex Morrall

The girl who sits near the blackboard has long dark curls like the sister I left behind in my home country. She is taller than the rest of us. She walks around the playground playing with a silver chain about her neck, followed by a troupe of girls. I want to know what they are talking about. They seem so much like my order sister. I try to walk near them.

"And Ben said that he never played kiss chase ever, even though he did and I caught him. And I thought, well that's such a lie."

There is a general breath of agreement from her friends. "It's such a lie, Tanya. I remember he was playing."

Tanya continues her investigation into Ben's behaviour. No one seems to have noticed that I have joined them.

Suddenly one of Tanya's friends turns to face me. She stops and prevents me from following. I look hopelessly at the back of Tanya's curls.

"Do you want her following us around, Tanya?"

She pauses and barely glances in my direction. "Oh, you know, let her if she wants."

I beam with pleasure. Filled with confidence, I am sure that Tanya must be just like my sister. "Are you going to be a model when you grow up?" I ask. Remembering my sister's stated ambition.

Tanya smiles. "Hm, a model. Maybe. I want to be a singer really."

She turns and carries on walking.

"What sort of singer?"

"You ask a lot of questions."

I trail after Tanya for the next few days. I say, I like your beads. I let her borrow my coloured pencils with the line of cats drawn on them and don't say anything when she doesn't give them back. Tanya doesn't say anything about my accent. I keep looking for my sister in her, but the more I look, the more different she seems.

In class, we're learning electronics, linking the crocodile clips up to different objects to see which will make the bulb light up. Dave keeps wetting his finger to touch the knife in the network and then saying 'ouch'. "Nasty shock, that," he says every now and again before repeating the exercise and seeing how long he can hold onto the knife for. I think he's going to wear out the battery. "Try it," he tells me.

"Will it hurt?"

"Not really," he says, and then seems to think better of it. "Well, it did that time because I set it up differently. It's okay for me, though. I'm tough."

I can't see anything different in the circuit setup. I turn to look over at Tanya to see if I can see my sister's cheeky longing glinting out of the sides of her eyes, something that I haven't seen for months now. Tanya sees me looking and I flick my eyes away.

Dave is connecting the crocodile clips to either side of a plastic ruler. He flicks the bulb a few times. "S'broken," he says. "Stupid experiment."

"It's because it's plastic."

Dave scowls. "Don't be stupid." He pulls the ruler out of the circuit. "What do girls know about science?"

"Well we know that some things won't let the bulb light up, otherwise we wouldn't be doing the experiment."

"It's the things with funny shapes that stop the electricity, stupid. Like the apple."

I look at Dave for a couple of seconds. He's already bored of the conversation, leaning back onto the back two legs of his chair to check if his friend Brett at the other desk will catch his eye. He really seems to think that the apple does not conduct electricity because it is not the same shape as the other things on the circuit board.

The days are getting damp and grey. The bell goes and the teachers decide that it is not wet enough for us to stay indoors. I feel stressed that we can't stay in and read comics. It's easier to read about the two-dimensional girls who worry about losing their bionic powers than to watch Tanya, while I try to bleed her dry of every instance of her personality which reminds me of my lost sister.

We tend to start our march around the playground at the small fence by the fire exit from the Hall. Tanya is standing there with her hands against the fence, wearing jeans and a pink Disney top. I smile and walk over.

"You can't come and walk with us today," she says.

I don't understand. "Why?"

"Because you can't." She nods regally. "Learn to obey your elders and betters."

She starts walking away. I start to follow her anyway because I don't know where else to go. If my sister hadn't drowned, I think, I could have found her in the playground now. One of Tanya's followers turns to me, arms folded. As she gets closer she pushes me so hard, I lose my footing. I don't hit the ground, but I am scared enough to turn away. "Stupid girl, always staring," hisses the follower.

Tanya thinks I stared at her too much, then.

It rains completely the following day. I am relieved. And when it doesn't rain the next day, I ask to stay in and play with the circuit boards again. The circuit boards don't need words, the concepts fit no matter what language you want to talk about it in. And their rules are always the same. Mrs Taylor looks at me slightly pityingly, before giving her permission.

Looking for a book to get lost in

Looking for a book to get lost in?

Read Alex Morrall's "Helen and the Grandbees" - *A novel readers won't soon forget (Awais Khan)*.
Read THE FIRST THREE CHAPTERS FOR **FREE** HERE:
www.alexmorrall.com/free/

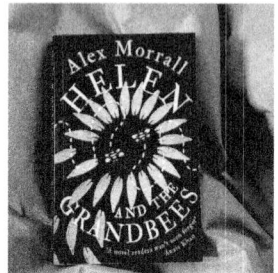

Twenty years ago, Helen is forced to give up her newborn baby, Lily. Now living alone in her small flat, there is a knock at the door and her bee, her Lily, is standing in front of her.

Reuniting means the world to them both, but Lily has questions. Lots of them. Questions that Helen is unwilling to answer. In turn Helen watches helplessly as her headstrong daughter launches from relationship to relationship, from kind Andrew, the father of her daughter, to violent Kingsley who fathers her son.

When it's clear her grandbees are in danger, tangled up in her daughter's damaging relationship, Helen must find the courage to step in, confronting the fears that haunt her the most.

Told in Helen's quirky voice *Helen and the Grandbees* addresses matters of identity, race and mental illness.

http://mybook.to/HelenandtheGrandbee

Author Bios

AUTHOR BIOs

Man Booker Prize shortlisted Clare Morrall shot to fame in a true to life rags-to-riches story when her novel 'Astonishing Splashes of Colour' and her tiny, unknown publisher became front page news after the shortlisting. Later novels have featured on TV Book Club, Front Row and Woman's Hour on Radio Four and Radio Three, along with the sale of film and foreign rights.

Alex Morrall is an artist and food blogger living in London. Her debut novel Helen and the Grandbees has been received as 'engaging and uplifting' by the national press.

Some of the people and worlds in these short stories appear in other Morrall books.

Sign up to the reading club to be kept up to date with new novels, reviews and inspirations by the Morralls on www.alexmorrall.com/free

'Breathtaking and moving, *Helen and the Grandbees* is a novel that bravely explores themes of familial discord, race and love in modern Britain. It is a book that immediately gripped me, compelling me to keep turning the pages well into the night. Morrall writes with confidence, poise, and a sense of humour to match. At times heartbreaking and heartwarming, this is a novel readers won't soon forget. A riveting debut.' *Awais Khan, author of In the Company of Strangers*

'Alex can write; she has a way, a bit like playwright Mike Leigh, of zooming into the tiniest, seemingly mundane physical details of a situation, and in so doing, conveying the complexity, circularity and pattern of relationship and emotion. There is a humanity and a realism about her writing that Is far from commonplace despite the fact that when you read about the people and situations in her storytelling, they are instantly recognisable. *Helen and the Grandbees* is unbearably sad but because Alex manages the seemingly impossible feat of introducing hope right from the start it is possible to read and read on, with curiosity and enjoyment.' *Dr Kairen Cullen, Writer and Psychologist*

'Authentic and tender. This utterly moving novel has created an unforgettable heroine in Helen. I held my breath as her troubled life unfolded and wanted only the best for her and her grandbees. This

gorgeous book is not just an exploration of identity, race and mental health, but also one about family love, sacrifice and bravery. I loved it.'
Carmel Harrington, International Bestselling Author

'What an honor and privilege it has been to read *Helen and the Grandbees*. I enjoyed it immensely. Every single character was memorable and felt completely genuine. Alex Morrall is a hugely talented author, with a gift for drawing characters of vastly different ages and from various backgrounds and social classes... This is the type of novel that will stick with me for a long time.' *Mary Rowen, author of Leaving the Beach*

Read the first three chapters of Alex Morrall's debut novel HELEN AND THE GRANDBEES for free here: Read THE FIRST THREE CHAPTERS FOR **FREE** HERE: www.alexmorrall.com/free

* * *

Printed in Great Britain
by Amazon